The MAGIC Crayon

Amy Sparkes ★ Ali Pye

PUFFIN

For Chloe, with love – A.S.

For Michael – A.P.

5% of author royalties are being donated to Ickle Pickles Children's Charity
www.icklepickles.org
Reg. charity number: 1129763

PUFFIN BOOKS

UK | USA | Canada | Ireland | Australia | India | New Zealand | South Africa

Puffin Books is part of the Penguin Random House group of companies whose addresses can be found at global.penguinrandomhouse.com.

www.penguin.co.uk www.puffin.co.uk www.ladybird.co.uk

Penguin Random House UK

First published 2020

001

Printed in China

A CIP catalogue record for this book is available from the British Library

ISBN: 978-0-141-37898-5

All correspondence to:
Puffin Books, Penguin Random House Children's,
One Embassy Gardens, New Union Square
5 Nine Elms Lane, London SW8 5DA

FSC www.fsc.org MIX Paper from responsible sources FSC® C018179

Jack was seven, and Chloe was six.
Jack liked his sister but **loved** to play tricks.

Once he tipped porridge down Chloe's new dress . . .

. . . and Chloe was
blamed for the
terrible mess!

So she sat in her room,
and she tried not to cry.

What was THAT?

All at once something
strange
caught her eye.

Her silvery crayon – there,
on the floor!
It **shone** and it sparkled
like never before . . .

"How strange," Chloe said, "but I know what to draw –
a horrid old witch outside Jack's bedroom door.

She'll soon sort him out
with a wave of her wand,
and change him to something
to put in her pond!"

She scribbled a witch with a tall, pointy hat,
and at once, at her door, came a **RAT-A-TAT-TAT!**

"Who's there?" Chloe said as the door opened wide . . .

. . . and the witch
from her picture
stepped quickly inside!

"Thanks for the frog," said the witch with a smile.
"I've wanted a pet for a very long while!"

But Chloe just stared. "My picture's come true?"
The witch rolled her eyes. "It's what magic things do!
Now come, Froggie-Jack.
You must hop on my broom."

Then she zapped at the ceiling
and **ZOOMed** from the room!

Now Chloe felt awful.
"I'm **SO** sorry, Jack!
Oh, what can I do?
I **MUST** get you back!"

With her silvery crayon,
she drew in the air,
and in sparkles of magic . . .

. . . a ladder was there!

Slowly at first, Chloe started to climb.
But she couldn't be nervous –
there just wasn't time . . .

She **climbed**
and she **climbed**
as fast as she could,

till she found herself in . . .

. . . a fairy-tale wood!

She crept through the wood
with the greatest of care.
(She had read all the stories and knew to beware!)

"Oh, where has that witch
taken Jack?" Chloe said,
when a shadowy shape appeared right ahead!

The **BIG BAD WOLF** grinned.
"A pleasure to meet you.
Though now I'm afraid that
I'm going to **eat you!**
I'm bored to the teeth,
and a meal will be fun."

But then Chloe's crayon shone bright as the sun . . .

With silvery speed, Chloe started to draw.
Would the magic work now as it had done before?

"Don't eat me!" she said. "Oh, please don't be mean.
If you're bored, have a go on this . . .

. . . WOLF TRAMPOLINE!"

The wolf jumped with joy, bouncing high in the sky.

And, taking her chance, Chloe tiptoed on by.

“Oh, where is that witch?”
Chloe said as she crept,
when into her path,
a **MASSIVE** foot stepped!

A **huge**, **stinky troll** with **huge**, **stinky feet**!

"I'm hungry!" he roared, "and ready to eat!"

He patted his belly with glee – but just then

Chloe noticed her crayon was shining again.

“Pooh!” Chloe coughed.
“You smell **REALLY** bad!
This Stink-Me-Not Perfume
will help – don’t be sad.”

She drew a big bottle –

the troll roared,

“HOORAY!

I’m a Stink-Me-Not Troll!”
And he started to spray.

So on tiptoed Chloe,
as hushed as a mouse,
when she saw
through the trees . . .

. . . a gingerbread house!

With a very deep breath,
Chloe crept down the path.
Then she heard **the witch** cackle,
"It's time for my bath!
Now be a good froggie
and sit on the floor."

As the witch went
KERSPLASH . . .

. . . Chloe crept through the door.

She snatched up her brother. "We really must dash,
Or that mean witch will turn us to bangers and mash!

Now I'll draw us a pony to help get us free."
But her lines were all bumpy – what would it be?

The shape had four legs and what looked like a horn . . .

"Hooray!" Chloe cried.

"It's our own unicorn!"

But what did they hear as they galloped away?

"MY FROGGIE IS GONE!"

yelled a voice in dismay.

And then came
the witch,
giving chase
through
the wood!

So down
clambered
Chloe as
fast as
she could!

The witch followed Chloe
back down to her room.

She **panted** and **puffed**,

"Should . . .
have . . .
taken . . .
my . . .
broom!

Enough of this nonsense!
Now give Froggie back!"

But Chloe said,
"**No!**
You must change
him to Jack."

“I wanted a pet,” sighed the witch, “just for me.”
And then Chloe’s crayon shone bright as can be.

“I have an idea
so you won’t be alone!
I’ll draw you a wonderful . . .

. . . pet of your own!"

The witch was delighted. "Oh, thank you for this!
Now, to get back your brother – give Froggie a kiss."

"Yuck!" Chloe said
as she kissed
the frog's nose.

"I know," shrugged
the witch.
"That's just **how**
magic goes."

There came
a bright

FLASH,

a **POP**

and a

CRACK . . .

And there stood her brother – "I'm sorry," said Jack.
"You saved me, although I've been so mean to you."

"I did," Chloe said.
"That's what **great** sisters do!"

"Righty-ho," said the witch.
"Toodleloo, both of you!"
Then she climbed up the ladder,
which vanished from view.

With a smile, Chloe tidied
her crayon away . . .

. . . where it quietly waits
for its next chance to play!